We Are Great!

An Ivy and Mack story

Written by Rebecca Colby
Illustrated by Gustavo Mazali

Collins

Who and what is in this story?

Listen and say 🎧 ①

Download the audio at www.collins.co.uk/839759

Ivy says, "Look, Mack. Photos! This book is about me."

Mack says, "And me!"

Ivy says, "In this photo, I'm six years old. I'm at school."

Mack says, "I'm four years old.
I'm at school, too."

Ivy says, "I'm old and you're young.
I can read."

Mack says, "I'm old, too. I can read."

Ivy says, "I'm big and you're small.
I'm holding you."

Mack says, "I'm big, too.
I'm holding you. I'm VERY big!"

Ivy says, "OK, but I'm tall. You're short."

Mack says, "No, I'm not short. Croc is short. He is very, VERY short."

Ivy says, "We are eating ice cream at the beach. Grandpa and I are clean. You're dirty."

Mack says, "Croc is dirty, too.
Croc LOVES ice cream."

Look at
Banjo the dog!

Ivy says, "These are great photos of us!"

Mack says, "These are funny photos of you!"

Ivy says, "You're funny, too. You're a funny brother!"

Mack asks, "Am I a good brother?"

Ivy says, "You are a GREAT brother!"

Mack says, "And you are a GREAT sister! We're a GREAT family!"

Picture dictionary

Listen and repeat

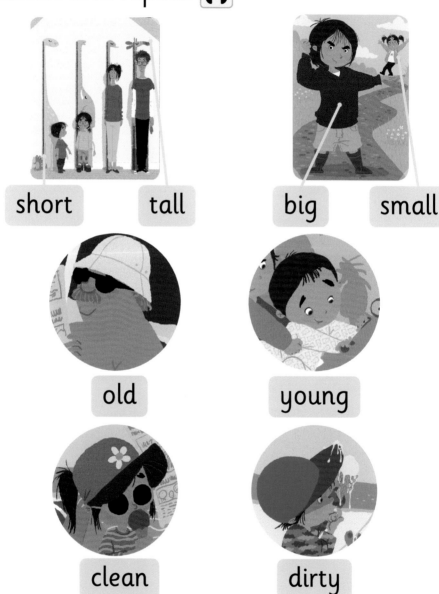

short   tall   big   small

old   young

clean   dirty

1 Look and order the story

2 Listen and say

Collins

Published by Collins
An imprint of HarperCollins*Publishers*
Westerhill Road
Bishopbriggs
Glasgow
G64 2QT

HarperCollins*Publishers*
Macken House, 39/40 Mayor Street Upper,
Dublin 1
DO1 C9W8
Ireland

William Collins' dream of knowledge for all began with the publication of his first book in 1819.

A self-educated mill worker, he not only enriched millions of lives, but also founded a flourishing publishing house. Today, staying true to this spirit, Collins books are packed with inspiration, innovation and practical expertise. They place you at the centre of a world of possibility and give you exactly what you need to explore it.

© HarperCollins*Publishers* Limited 2020

10 9 8 7 6 5 4 3

ISBN 978-0-00-839759-3

Collins® and COBUILD® are registered trademarks of HarperCollins*Publishers* Limited

www.collins.co.uk/elt

British Library Cataloguing in Publication Data

A catalogue record for this publication is available from the British Library.

Author: Rebecca Colby
Illustrator: Gustavo Mazali (Beehive)
Series editor: Rebecca Adlard
Publishing manager: Lisa Todd
Product managers: Jennifer Hall and Caroline Green
In-house editor: Alma Puts Keren
Project manager: Emily Hooton
Editor: Deborah Friedland
Proofreaders: Natalie Murray and Michael Lamb
Cover designer: Kevin Robbins
Typesetter: 2Hoots Publishing Services Ltd
Audio produced by id audio, London
Reading guide author: Julie Penn
Production controller: Rachel Weaver
Printed and bound in the UK by Pureprint

MIX
Paper | Supporting responsible forestry
FSC™ C007454
www.fsc.org

This book contains FSC™ certified paper and other controlled sources to ensure responsible forest management.

For more information visit: www.harpercollins.co.uk/green

Download the audio for this book and a reading guide for parents and teachers at www.collins.co.uk/839759